Squeakopotamus

Dawn McMillan

Illustrated by Ross Kinnaird

Oratia

Who's this in our house, munching toast and cheese?

Squeakopotamus!

Who's this at our table,
eating potatoes and peas?

Squeakopotamus!

And who's this on our sofa,
   cushions underneath his knees?

Of course you know ... it's Squeakopotamus!

Is he a hippo that
looks like a mouse?
Or is he a mouse
too big for this house?

Too big for this house? Then where will he stay?
We can't chase him out. It's raining today.

I want to keep him. He can be mine.
Mum says, 'No!' Dad says, 'Fine!'
Kate says nothing. She doesn't mind.

So ... who's my new pet?
Have you guessed yet?

Squeakopotamus!

I've said he can sleep on the floor by my bed.
He's taken my pillows for under his head!

Who's rattling and roaring?

Snorting and snoring?

Squeakopotamus!

Someone's awake, licking his lips!
Rubbing his tummy, *wiggling* his hips!

He's tapping his feet.
He wants something to eat!

We've run out of cheese!
　　No more potatoes or peas!

My heart starts to race.
I feel the blood in my face.
My head's in a fuss.

Maybe Squeakopotamus
wants to *eat ... us!*

We're out of here at

lightning speed!

Off to the market
  to get what we need.

Now ... who's getting bored?
Who wants to play?
Who doesn't care about rain on this day?

The wet wind is blowing.
But it seems that we're going with ...

Squeakopotamus!

No raincoat to fit him.
No umbrella so tall.
No boots for his feet.
Everything is too small.

Who's getting wet?

Squeakopotamus!

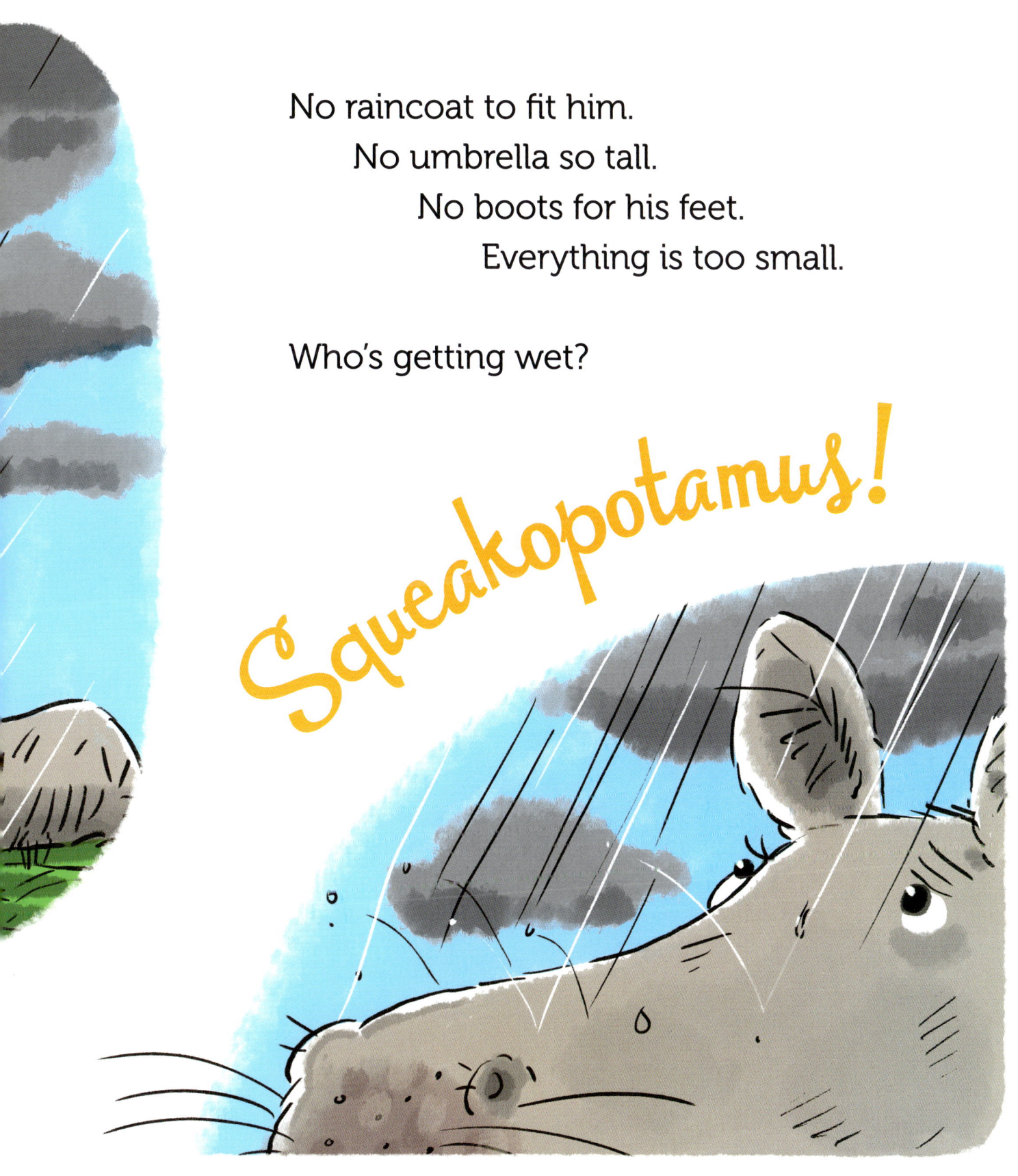

he's down to mouse size!

And Mum says, 'Thank goodness!
'A downsized Squeako is easy to keep.
'He'll live in a cage. His food will be cheap!'
Kate is relieved. She'll get some sleep.

But Dad and I ... we share our regret
because no one yet
has *ever* had a pet
like our ...

astonishing,

 *astounding,*

demolishing,

confounding...

Squeakopotamus!

About the author

Hi there! I'm Dawn McMillan from down by the sea, on the Coromandel Peninsula in New Zealand. I live with my husband and our cat, both normal size. Among the other tall tales Ross and I have published together are *Why do Dogs Sniff Bottoms?*, *Doctor Grundy's Undies*, *Mister Spears and his Hairy Ears*, and *I Need a New Bum!*

About the illustrator

Gidday. I'm Ross Kinnaird. I'm an illustrator and a graphic designer and I live in Auckland. When I'm not illustrating a book or being cross with my computer, I enjoy most activities to do with the sea. I love visiting schools to talk about books and drawing. (I've been known to draw some really funny cartoons of the teachers!)

Published by Oratia Books, Oratia Media Ltd,
783 West Coast Road, Oratia, Auckland 0604, New Zealand (www.oratia.co.nz).

Copyright © 2016 Dawn McMillan — text
Copyright © 2016 Ross Kinnaird — illustrations
Copyright © 2016 Oratia Books (published work)

The copyright holders assert their moral rights in the work.

This book is copyright. Except for the purposes of fair reviewing, no part of this publication may be reproduced or transmitted in any form or by any means, whether electronic, digital or mechanical, including photocopying, recording, any digital or computerised format, or any information storage and retrieval system, including by any means via the Internet, without permission in writing from the publisher. Infringers of copyright render themselves liable to prosecution.

ISBN 978-0-947506-11-7

First published 2016
Printed in China